Medea

DOVER · THRIFT · EDITIONS

Medea

EURIPIDES

TRANSLATED BY REX WARNER

DOVER PUBLICATIONS, INC.
New York

DOVER THRIFT EDITIONS

Editor: Stanley Appelbaum

Performance

This Dover Thrift Edition may be used in its entirety, in adaptation or in any other way for theatrical productions, professional and amateur, in the United States, without fee, permission or acknowledgment. (This may not apply outside of the United States, as copyright conditions may vary.)

This Dover edition, first published in 1993, is an unabridged republication of the translation by Rex Warner originally published by John Lane, The Bodley Head Limited, London, in 1944. A new Note and explanatory footnotes have been prepared specially for the present edition.

Manufactured in the United States of America
Dover Publications, Inc., 31 East 2nd Street, Mineola, N.Y. 11501

Library of Congress Cataloging-in-Publication Data

Euripides.
   [Medea. English]
   Medea / Euripides ; translated by Rex Warner.
      p.   cm. — (Dover thrift editions)
   ISBN 0-486-27548-5 (pbk.)
   1. Medea (Greek mythology)—Drama.   I. Warner, Rex, 1905–   II. Title.
III. Series.
PA3975.M4W34   1993
882'.01—dc20
                                                                                    92-31819
                                                                                           CIP

Note

Younger than Aeschylus and Sophocles, Euripides (ca. 485 to ca. 406 B.C.) was the last of the great writers of tragedy in the golden age of Athens, and the most influential on later playwrights from ancient to modern times. His emphasis on human emotions and individual psychology has proved more widely popular than the philosophical reflections of his older contemporaries. *Medea*, first produced in 431 B.C., features strong dramatic situations and a stirring part for the heroine, whose attitude of feminine pride and revolt against tradition still strikes a very modern note.

A few explanatory footnotes have been added to the present edition of Rex Warner's very straightforward and readable translation.

Characters

MEDEA, *princess of Colchis and wife of*

JASON, *son of* AESON, *king of Iolcus*

Two children of MEDEA *and* JASON

CREON, *king of Corinth*

AEGEUS, *king of Athens*

NURSE *to* MEDEA

TUTOR *to* MEDEA's *children*

MESSENGER

CHORUS *of Corinthian Women*

Medea

SCENE: *In front of Medea's house in Corinth. Enter from the house Medea's nurse.*

NURSE   How I wish the Argo* never had reached the land
Of Colchis, skimming through the blue Symplegades,
Nor ever had fallen in the glades of Pelion·
The smitten fir-tree to furnish oars for the hands
Of heroes who in Pelias' name attempted
The Golden Fleece! For then my mistress Medea
Would not have sailed for the towers of the land of Iolcus,
Her heart on fire with passionate love for Jason;
Nor would she have persuaded the daughters of Pelias
To kill their father, and now be living here
In Corinth with her husband and children. She gave
Pleasure to the people of her land of exile,
And she herself helped Jason in every way.
This is indeed the greatest salvation of all—
For the wife not to stand apart from the husband.
But now there's hatred everywhere, Love is diseased.
For, deserting his own children and my mistress,
Jason has taken a royal wife to his bed,
The daughter of the ruler of this land, Creon.
And poor Medea is slighted, and cries aloud on the
Vows they made to each other, the right hands clasped

---

* Jason's ship on the expedition of the Argonauts, sent by Pelias, king of Iolcus in Thessaly (Jason's uncle, who had usurped the throne), to Colchis on the Black Sea. The Symplegades were clashing rocks, one of the obstacles along the way. Pelion is a mountain in Thessaly. Medea was a princess of Colchis who fell in love with Jason and followed him back to Greece.

In eternal promise. She calls upon the gods to witness
What sort of return Jason has made to her love.
She lies without food and gives herself up to suffering,
Wasting away every moment of the day in tears.
So it has gone since she knew herself slighted by him.
Not stirring an eye, not moving her face from the ground,
No more than either a rock or surging sea water
She listens when she is given friendly advice.
Except that sometimes she twists back her white neck and
Moans to herself, calling out on her father's name,
And her land, and her home betrayed when she came away with
A man who now is determined to dishonor her.
Poor creature, she has discovered by her sufferings
What it means to one not to have lost one's own country.
She has turned from the children and does not like to see them.
I am afraid she may think of some dreadful thing,
For her heart is violent. She will never put up with
The treatment she is getting. I know and fear her
Lest she may sharpen a sword and thrust to the heart,
Stealing into the palace where the bed is made,
Or even kill the king and the new-wedded groom,
And thus bring a greater misfortune on herself.
She's a strange woman. I know it won't be easy
To make an enemy of her and come off best.
But here the children come. They have finished playing.
They have no thought at all of their mother's trouble.
Indeed it is not usual for the young to grieve.

(*Enter from the right the slave who is the tutor to Medea's two small children. The children follow him.*)

TUTOR You old retainer of my mistress' household,
Why are you standing here all alone in front of the
Gates and moaning to yourself over your misfortune?
Medea could not wish you to leave her alone.

NURSE	Old man, and guardian of the children of Jason,
	If one is a good servant, it's a terrible thing
	When one's master's luck is out; it goes to one's heart.
	So I myself have got into such a state of grief
	That a longing stole over me to come outside here
	And tell the earth and air of my mistress' sorrows.
TUTOR	Has the poor lady not yet given up her crying?
NURSE	Given up? She's at the start, not halfway through her tears.
TUTOR	Poor fool—if I may call my mistress such a name—
	How ignorant she is of trouble more to come.
NURSE	What do you mean, old man? You needn't fear to speak.
TUTOR	Nothing. I take back the words which I used just now.
NURSE	Don't, by your beard, hide this from me, your fellow-servant.
	If need be, I'll keep quiet about what you tell me.
TUTOR	I heard a person saying, while I myself seemed
	Not to be paying attention, when I was at the place
	Where the old draught-players sit, by the holy fountain,
	That Creon, ruler of the land, intends to drive
	These children and their mother in exile from Corinth.
	But whether what he said is really true or not
	I do not know. I pray that it may not be true.
NURSE	And will Jason put up with it that his children
	Should suffer so, though he's no friend to their mother?
TUTOR	Old ties give place to new ones. As for Jason, he
	No longer has a feeling for this house of ours.
NURSE	It's black indeed for us, when we add new to old
	Sorrows before even the present sky has cleared.
TUTOR	But you be silent, and keep all this to yourself.
	It is not the right time to tell our mistress of it.

NURSE Do you hear, children, what a father he is to you?
       I wish he were dead—but no, he is still my master.
       Yet certainly he has proved unkind to his dear ones.

TUTOR What's strange in that? Have you only just discovered
       That everyone loves himself more than his neighbor?
       Some have good reason, others get something out of it.
       So Jason neglects his children for the new bride.

NURSE Go indoors, children. That will be the best thing.
       And you, keep them to themselves as much as possible.
       Don't bring them near their mother in her angry mood.
       For I've seen her already blazing her eyes at them
       As though she meant some mischief and I am sure that
       She'll not stop raging until she has struck at someone.
       May it be an enemy and not a friend she hurts!

(Medea is heard inside the house.)

MEDEA Ah, wretch! Ah, lost in my sufferings,
       I wish, I wish I might die.

NURSE What did I say, dear children? Your mother
       Frets her heart and frets it to anger.
       Run away quickly into the house,
       And keep well out of her sight.
       Don't go anywhere near, but be careful
       Of the wildness and bitter nature
       Of that proud mind.
       Go now! Run quickly indoors.
       It is clear that she soon will put lightning
       In that cloud of her cries that is rising
       With a passion increasing. O, what will she do,
       Proud-hearted and not to be checked on her course,
       A soul bitten into with wrong?

(The Tutor takes the children into the house.)

MEDEA   Ah, I have suffered
        What should be wept for bitterly. I hate you,
        Children of a hateful mother. I curse you
        And your father. Let the whole house crash.

NURSE   Ah, I pity you, you poor creature.
        How can your children share in their father's
        Wickedness? Why do you hate them? Oh children,
        How much I fear that something may happen!
        Great people's tempers are terrible, always
        Having their own way, seldom checked,
        Dangerous they shift from mood to mood.
        How much better to have been accustomed
        To live on equal terms with one's neighbors.
        I would like to be safe and grow old in a
        Humble way. What is moderate sounds best,
        Also in practice *is* best for everyone.
        Greatness brings no profit to people.
        God indeed, when in anger, brings
        Greater ruin to great men's houses.

>   (*Enter, on the right, a Chorus of Corinthian women. They have come to inquire about Medea and to attempt to console her.*)

CHORUS I heard the voice, I heard the cry
        Of Colchis' wretched daughter.
        Tell me, mother, is she not yet
        At rest? Within the double gates
        Of the court I heard her cry. I am sorry
        For the sorrow of this home. O, say, what has happened?

NURSE   There is no home. It's over and done with.
        Her husband holds fast to his royal wedding,
        While she, my mistress, cries out her eyes
        There in her room, and takes no warmth from
        Any word of any friend.

MEDEA   Oh, I wish
         That lightning from heaven would split my head open.
         Oh, what use have I now for life?
         I would find my release in death
         And leave hateful existence behind me.

CHORUS   O God and Earth and Heaven!
         Did you hear what a cry was that
         Which the sad wife sings?
         Poor foolish one, why should you long
         For that appalling rest?
         The final end of death comes fast.
         No need to pray for that.
         Suppose your man gives honor
         To another woman's bed.
         It often happens. Don't be hurt.
         God will be your friend in this.
         You must not waste away
         Grieving too much for him who shared your bed.

MEDEA   Great Themis, lady Artemis,* behold
         The things I suffer, though I made him promise,
         My hateful husband. I pray that I may see him,
         Him and his bride and all their palace shattered
         For the wrong they dare to do me without cause.
         Oh, my father! Oh, my country! In what dishonor
         I left you, killing my own brother for it.**

NURSE   Do you hear what she says, and how she cries
         On Themis, the goddess of Promises, and on Zeus,
         Whom we believe to be the Keeper of Oaths?
         Of this I am sure, that no small thing
         Will appease my mistress' anger.

---

  * Goddesses: Themis was the goddess of justice, the virgin Artemis would be sensitive to the plight of women.

  ** During the escape from Colchis, to delay her father's pursuit.

CHORUS   Will she come into our presence?
         Will she listen when we are speaking
         To the words we say?
         I wish she might relax her rage
         And temper of her heart.
         My willingness to help will never
         Be wanting to my friends.
         But go inside and bring her
         Out of the house to us,
         And speak kindly to her: hurry,
         Before she wrongs her own.
         This passion of hers moves to something great.

NURSE   I will, but I doubt if I'll manage
         To win my mistress over.
         But still I'll attempt it to please you.
         Such a look she will flash on her servants
         If any comes near with a message,
         Like a lioness guarding her cubs.
         It is right, I think, to consider
         Both stupid and lacking in foresight
         Those poets of old who wrote songs
         For revels and dinners and banquets,
         Pleasant sounds for men living at ease;
         But none of them all has discovered
         How to put to an end with their singing
         Or musical instruments grief,
         Bitter grief, from which death and disaster
         Cheat the hopes of a house. Yet how good
         If music could cure men of this! But why raise
         To no purpose the voice at a banquet? For *there* is
         Already abundance of pleasure for men
         With a joy of its own.

(The Nurse goes into the house.)

CHORUS   I heard a shriek that is laden with sorrow.
Shrilling out her hard grief she cries out
Upon him who betrayed both her bed and her marriage.
Wronged, she calls on the gods,
On the justice of Zeus, the oath sworn,
Which brought her away
To the opposite shore of the Greeks
Through the gloomy salt straits to the gateway
Of the salty unlimited sea.

(Medea, attended by servants, comes out of the house.)

MEDEA   Women of Corinth, I have come outside to you
Lest you should be indignant with me; for I know
That many people are overproud, some when alone,
And others when in company. And those who live
Quietly, as I do, get a bad reputation.
For a just judgment is not evident in the eyes
When a man at first sight hates another, before
Learning his character, being in no way injured;
And a foreigner especially must adapt himself.
I'd not approve of even a fellow-countryman
Who by pride and want of manners offends his neighbors.
But on me this thing has fallen so unexpectedly,
It has broken my heart. I am finished. I let go
All my life's joy. My friends, I only want to die.
It was everything to me to think well of one man,
And he, my own husband, has turned out wholly vile.
Of all things which are living and can form a judgment
We women are the most unfortunate creatures.
Firstly, with an excess of wealth it is required
For us to buy a husband and take for our bodies
A master; for not to take one is even worse.
And now the question is serious whether we take
A good or bad one; for there is no easy escape
For a woman, nor can she say no to her marriage.
She arrives among new modes of behavior and manners,

And needs prophetic power, unless she has learned at
  home,
How best to manage him who shares the bed with her.
And if we work out all this well and carefully,
And the husband lives with us and lightly bears his yoke,
Then life is enviable. If not, I'd rather die.
A man, when he's tired of the company in his home,
Goes out of the house and puts an end to his boredom
And turns to a friend or companion of his own age.
But we are forced to keep our eyes on one alone.
What they say of us is that we have a peaceful time
Living at home, while they do the fighting in war.
How wrong they are! I would very much rather stand
Three times in the front of battle than bear one child.
Yet what applies to me does not apply to you.
You have a country. Your family home is here.
You enjoy life and the company of your friends.
But I am deserted, a refugee, thought nothing of
By my husband—something he won in a foreign land.
I have no mother or brother, nor any relation
With whom I can take refuge in this sea of woe.
This much then is the service I would beg from you:
If I can find the means or devise any scheme
To pay my husband back for what he has done to me—
Him and his father-in-law and the girl who married him—
Just to keep silent. For in other ways a woman
Is full of fear, defenseless, dreads the sight of cold
Steel; but, when once she is wronged in the matter of love,
No other soul can hold so many thoughts of blood.

CHORUS This I will promise. You are in the right, Medea,
In paying your husband back. I am not surprised at you
For being sad.
            But look! I see our King Creon
Approaching. He will tell us of some new plan.

            (Enter, from the right, Creon, with attendants.)

CREON   You, with that angry look, so set against your husband,
        Medea, I order you to leave my territories
        An exile, and take along with you your two children,
        And not to waste time doing it. It is my decree,
        And I will see it done. I will not return home
        Until you are cast from the boundaries of my land.

MEDEA   Oh, this is the end for me. I am utterly lost.
        Now I am in the full force of the storm of hate
        And have no harbor from ruin to reach easily.
        Yet still, in spite of it all, I'll ask the question:
        What is your reason, Creon, for banishing me?

CREON   I am afraid of you—why should I dissemble it?—
        Afraid that you may injure my daughter mortally.
        Many things accumulate to support my feeling.
        You are a clever woman, versed in evil arts,
        And are angry at having lost your husband's love.
        I hear that you are threatening, so they tell me,
        To do something against my daughter and Jason
        And me, too. I shall take my precautions first.
        I tell you, I prefer to earn your hatred now
        Than to be soft-hearted and afterward regret it.

MEDEA   This is not the first time, Creon. Often previously
        Through being considered clever I have suffered much.
        A person of sense ought never to have his children
        Brought up to be more clever than the average.
        For, apart from cleverness bringing them no profit,
        It will make them objects of envy and ill-will.
        If you put new ideas before the eyes of fools
        They'll think you foolish and worthless into the bargain;
        And if you are thought superior to those who have
        Some reputation for learning, you will become hated.
        I have some knowledge myself of how this happens;
        For being clever, I find that some will envy me,
        Others object to me. Yet all my cleverness

                    Is not so much.
                                    Well, then, are you frightened, Creon,
                    That I should harm you? There is no need. It is not
                    My way to transgress the authority of a king.
                    How have you injured me? You gave your daughter away
                    To the man you wanted. Oh, certainly I hate
                    My husband, but you, I think, have acted wisely;
                    Nor do I grudge it you that your affairs go well.
                    May the marriage be a lucky one! Only let me
                    Live in this land. For even though I have been wronged,
                    I will not raise my voice, but submit to my betters.

CREON   What you say sounds gentle enough. Still in my heart
        I greatly dread that you are plotting some evil,
        And therefore I trust you even less than before.
        A sharp-tempered woman, or, for that matter, a man,
        Is easier to deal with than the clever type
        Who holds her tongue. No. You must go. No need for more
        Speeches. The thing is fixed. By no manner of means
        Shall you, an enemy of mine, stay in my country.

MEDEA   I beg you. By your knees, by your new-wedded girl.

CREON   Your words are wasted. You will never persuade me.

MEDEA   Will you drive me out, and give no heed to my prayers?

CREON   I will, for I love my family more than you.

MEDEA   O my country! How bitterly now I remember you!

CREON   I love my country too—next after my children.

MEDEA   Oh what an evil to men is passionate love!

CREON   That would depend on the luck that goes along with it.

MEDEA   O God, do not forget who is the cause of this!

CREON   Go. It is no use. Spare me the pain of forcing you.

MEDEA   I'm spared no pain. I lack no pain to be spared me.

CREON   Then you'll be removed by force by one of my men.

MEDEA   No, Creon, not that! But do listen, I beg you.

CREON   Woman, you seem to want to create a disturbance.

MEDEA   I *will* go into exile. *This* is not what I beg for.

CREON   Why then this violence and clinging to my hand?

MEDEA   Allow me to remain here just for this one day,
So I may consider where to live in my exile,
And look for support for my children, since their father
Chooses to make no kind of provision for them.
Have pity on them! You have children of your own.
It is natural for you to look kindly on them.
For myself I do not mind if I go into exile.
It is the children being in trouble that I mind.

CREON   There is nothing tyrannical about my nature,
And by showing mercy I have often been the loser.
Even now I know that I am making a mistake.
All the same you shall have your will. But this I tell you,
That if the light of heaven tomorrow shall see you,
You and your children in the confines of my land,
You die. This word I have spoken is firmly fixed.
But now, if you must stay, stay for this day alone.
For in it you can do none of the things I fear.

(Exit Creon with his attendants.)

CHORUS   Oh, unfortunate one! Oh, cruel!
Where will you turn? Who will help you?
What house or what land to preserve you
From ill can you find?
Medea, a god has thrown suffering
Upon you in waves of despair.

MEDEA   Things have gone badly every way. No doubt of that.
But not these things this far, and don't imagine so.
There are still trials to come for the new-wedded pair,
And for their relations pain that will mean something.
Do you think that I would ever have fawned on that man

Unless I had some end to gain or profit in it?
I would not even have spoken or touched him with my
  hands.
But he has got to such a pitch of foolishness
That, though he could have made nothing of all my plans
By exiling me, he has given me this one day
To stay here, and in this I will make dead bodies
Of three of my enemies—father, the girl, and my husband.
I have many ways of death which I might suit to them,
And do not know, friends, which one to take in hand;
Whether to set fire underneath their bridal mansion,
Or sharpen a sword and thrust it to the heart,
Stealing into the palace where the bed is made.
There is just one obstacle to this. If I am caught
Breaking into the house and scheming against it,
I shall die, and give my enemies cause for laughter.
It is best to go by the straight road, the one in which
I am most skilled, and make away with them by poison.
So be it then.
And now suppose them dead. What town will receive me?
What friend will offer me a refuge in his land,
Or the guaranty of his house and save my own life?
There is none. So I must wait a little time yet,
And if some sure defense should then appear for me,
In craft and silence I will set about this murder.
But if my fate should drive me on without help,
Even though death is certain, I will take the sword
Myself and kill, and steadfastly advance to crime.
It shall not be—I swear it by her, my mistress,
Whom most I honor and have chosen as partner,
Hecate,* who dwells in the recesses of my hearth—
That any man shall be glad to have injured me.
Bitter I will make their marriage for them and mournful,
Bitter the alliance and the driving me out of the land.

---

* A goddess of the night.

Ah, come, Medea, in your plotting and scheming
Leave nothing untried of all those things which you know.
Go forward to the dreadful act. The test has come
For resolution. You see how you are treated. Never
Shall you be mocked by Jason's Corinthian wedding,
Whose father was noble, whose grandfather Helius.*
You have the skill. What is more, you were born a woman,
And women, though most helpless in doing good deeds,
Are of every evil the cleverest of contrivers.

CHORUS   Flow backward to your sources, sacred rivers,
And let the world's great order be reversed.
It is the thoughts of *men* that are deceitful,
Their pledges that are loose.
Story shall now turn my condition to a fair one,
Women are paid their due.
No more shall evil-sounding fame be theirs.

Cease now, you muses of the ancient singers,
To tell the tale of my unfaithfulness;
For not on us did Phoebus, lord of music,**
Bestow the lyre's divine
Power, for otherwise I should have sung an answer
To the other sex. Long time
Has much to tell of us, and much of them.

You sailed away from your father's home,
With a heart on fire you passed
The double rocks of the sea.
And now in a foreign country
You have lost your rest in a widowed bed,
And are driven forth, a refugee
In dishonor from the land.

Good faith has gone, and no more remains
In great Greece a sense of shame.

* Sun god.
** Apollo.

It has flown away to the sky.
No father's house for a haven
Is at hand for you now, and another queen
Of your bed has dispossessed you and
Is mistress of your home.

(Enter Jason, with attendants.)

JASON   This is not the first occasion that I have noticed
How hopeless it is to deal with a stubborn temper.
For, with reasonable submission to our ruler's will,
You might have lived in this land and kept your home.
As it is you are going to be exiled for your loose speaking.
Not that I mind myself. You are free to continue
Telling everyone that Jason is a worthless man.
But as to your talk about the king, consider
Yourself most lucky that exile is your punishment.
I, for my part, have always tried to calm down
The anger of the king, and wished you to remain.
But you will not give up your folly, continually
Speaking ill of him, and so you are going to be banished.
All the same, and in spite of your conduct, I'll not desert
My friends, but have come to make some provision for you,
So that you and the children may not be penniless
Or in need of anything in exile. Certainly
Exile brings many troubles with it. And even
If you hate me, I cannot think badly of you.

MEDEA   O coward in every way—that is what I call you,
With bitterest reproach for your lack of manliness,
You have come, you, my worst enemy, have come to me!
It is not an example of overconfidence
Or of boldness thus to look your friends in the face,
Friends you have injured—no, it is the worst of all
Human diseases, shamelessness. But you did well
To come, for I can speak ill of you and lighten
My heart, and you will suffer while you are listening.
And first I will begin from what happened first.

I saved your life, and every Greek knows I saved it,
Who was a shipmate of yours aboard the Argo,
When you were sent to control the bulls that breathed fire
And yoke them, and when you would sow that deadly field.
Also that snake, who encircled with his many folds
The Golden Fleece and guarded it and never slept,
I killed, and so gave you the safety of the light.
And I myself betrayed my father and my home,
And came with you to Pelias' land of Iolcus.
And then, showing more willingness to help than wisdom,
I killed him, Pelias, with a most dreadful death
At his own daughters' hands, and took away your fear.
This is how I behaved to you, you wretched man,
And you forsook me, took another bride to bed,
Though you had children; for, if that had not been,
You would have had an excuse for another wedding.
Faith in your word has gone. Indeed, I cannot tell
Whether you think the gods whose names you swore by then
Have ceased to rule and that new standards are set up,
Since you must know you have broken your word to me.
O my right hand, and the knees which you often clasped
In supplication, how senselessly I am treated
By this bad man, and how my hopes have missed their mark!
Come, I will share my thoughts as though you were a friend—
You! Can I think that you would ever treat me well?
But I will do it, and these questions will make you
Appear the baser. Where am I to go? To my father's?
Him I betrayed and his land when I came with you.
To Pelias' wretched daughters? What a fine welcome
They would prepare for me who murdered their father!
For this is my position—hated by my friends
At home, I have, in kindness to you, made enemies
Of others whom there was no need to have injured.

>   And how happy among Greek women you have made me
>   On your side for all this! A distinguished husband
>   I have—for breaking promises. When in misery
>   I am cast out of the land and go into exile,
>   Quite without friends and all alone with my children,
>   That will be a fine shame for the new-wedded groom,
>   For his children to wander as beggars and she who saved him.
>   O God, you have given to mortals a sure method
>   Of telling the gold that is pure from the counterfeit;
>   Why is there no mark engraved upon men's bodies,
>   By which we could know the true ones from the false ones?
>
> CHORUS   It is a strange form of anger, difficult to cure,
>   When two friends turn upon each other in hatred.
>
> JASON   As for me, it seems I must be no bad speaker.
>   But, like a man who has a good grip of the tiller,
>   Reef up his sail, and so run away from under
>   This mouthing tempest, woman, of your bitter tongue.
>   Since you insist on building up your kindness to me,
>   My view is that Cypris* was alone responsible
>   Of men and gods for the preserving of my life.
>   You are clever enough—but really I need not enter
>   Into the story of how it was love's inescapable
>   Power that compelled you to keep my person safe.
>   On this I will not go into too much detail.
>   In so far as you helped me, you did well enough.
>   But on this question of saving me, I can prove
>   You have certainly got from me more than you gave.
>   Firstly, instead of living among barbarians,
>   You inhabit a Greek land and understand our ways,
>   How to live by law instead of the sweet will of force.
>   And all the Greeks considered you a clever woman.
>   You were honored for it; while, if you were living at

---

* Aphrodite, goddess of love.

The ends of the earth, nobody would have heard of you.
For my part, rather than stores of gold in my house
Or power to sing even sweeter songs than Orpheus,
I'd choose the fate that made me a distinguished man.
There is my reply to your story of my labors.
Remember it was you who started the argument.
Next for your attack on my wedding with the princess:
Here I will prove that, first, it was a clever move,
Secondly, a wise one, and, finally, that I made it
In your best interests and the children's. Please keep
    calm.
When I arrived here from the land of Iolcus,
Involved, as I was, in every kind of difficulty,
What luckier chance could I have come across than this,
An exile to marry the daughter of the king?
It was not—the point that seems to upset you—that I
Grew tired of your bed and felt the need of a new bride;
Nor with any wish to outdo your number of children.
We have enough already. I am quite content.
But—this was the main reason—that we might live well,
And not be short of anything. I know that all
A man's friends leave him stone-cold if he becomes poor.
Also that I might bring my children up worthily
Of my position, and, by producing more of them
To be brothers of yours, we would draw the families
Together and all be happy. You need no children.
And it pays me to do good to those I have now
By having others. Do you think this a bad plan?
You wouldn't if the love question hadn't upset you.
But you women have got into such a state of mind
That, if your life at night is good, you think you have
Everything; but, if in that quarter things go wrong,
You will consider your best and truest interests
Most hateful. It would have been better far for men
To have got their children in some other way, and women
Not to have existed. Then life would have been good.

CHORUS   Jason, though you have made this speech of yours look
           well,
         Still I think, even though others do not agree,
         You have betrayed your wife and are acting badly.

MEDEA   Surely in many ways I hold different views
         From others, for I think that the plausible speaker
         Who is a villain deserves the greatest punishment.
         Confident in his tongue's power to adorn evil,
         He stops at nothing. Yet he is not really wise.
         As in your case. There is no need to put on the airs
         Of a clever speaker, for one word will lay you flat.
         If you were not a coward, you would not have married
         Behind my back, but discussed it with me first.

JASON   And you, no doubt, would have furthered the proposal,
         If I had told you of it, you who even now
         Are incapable of controlling your bitter temper.

MEDEA   It was not that. No, you thought it was not respectable
         As you got on in years to have a foreign wife.

JASON   Make sure of this: it was not because of a woman
         I made the royal alliance in which I now live,
         But, as I said before, I wished to preserve you
         And breed a royal progeny to be brothers
         To the children I have now, a sure defense to us.

MEDEA   Let me have no happy fortune that brings pain with it,
         Or prosperity which is upsetting to the mind!

JASON   Change your ideas of what you want, and show more sense.
         Do not consider painful what is good for you,
         Nor, when you are lucky, think yourself unfortunate.

MEDEA   You can insult me. You have somewhere to turn to.
         But I shall go from this land into exile, friendless.

JASON   It was what you chose yourself. Don't blame others for it.

MEDEA   And how did I choose it? Did I betray my husband?

JASON   You called down wicked curses on the king's family.

MEDEA   A curse, that is what I am become to your house too.

JASON   I do not propose to go into all the rest of it;
         But, if you wish for the children or for yourself
         In exile to have some of my money to help you,
         Say so, for I am prepared to give with open hand,
         Or to provide you with introductions to my friends
         Who will treat you well. You are a fool if you do not
         Accept this. Cease your anger and you will profit.

MEDEA   I shall never accept the favors of friends of yours,
         Nor take a thing from you, so you need not offer it.
         There is no benefit in the gifts of a bad man.

JASON   Then, in any case, I call the gods to witness that
         I wish to help you and the children in every way,
         But you refuse what is good for you. Obstinately
         You push away your friends. You are sure to suffer for it.

MEDEA   Go! No doubt you hanker for your virginal bride,
         And are guilty of lingering too long out of her house.
         Enjoy your wedding. But perhaps—with the help of
            God—
         You will make the kind of marriage that you will regret.

                         (*Jason goes out with his attendants.*)

CHORUS   When love is in excess
         It brings a man no honor
         Nor any worthiness.
         But if in moderation Cypris comes,
         There is no other power at all so gracious.
         O goddess, never on me let loose the unerring
         Shaft of your bow in the poison of desire.

         Let my heart be wise.
         It is the gods' best gift.

On me let mighty Cypris
Inflict no wordy wars or restless anger
To urge my passion to a different love.
But with discernment may she guide women's weddings,
Honoring most what is peaceful in the bed.

O country and home,
Never, never may I be without you,
Living the hopeless life,
Hard to pass through and painful,
Most pitiable of all.
Let death first lay me low and death
Free me from this daylight.
There is no sorrow above
The loss of a native land.

I have seen it myself,
Do not tell of a secondhand story.
Neither city nor friend
Pitied you when you suffered
The worst of sufferings.
O let him die ungraced whose heart
Will not reward his friends,
Who cannot open an honest mind
No friend will he be of mine.

(Enter Aegeus, king of Athens, an old friend of Medea.)

AEGEUS   Medea, greeting! This is the best introduction
Of which men know for conversation between friends.

MEDEA   Greeting to you too, Aegeus, son of King Pandion.
Where have you come from to visit this country's soil?

AEGEUS   I have just left the ancient oracle of Phoebus.

MEDEA   And why did you go to earth's prophetic center?

AEGEUS   I went to inquire how children might be born to me.

MEDEA   Is it so? Your life still up to this point is childless?
AEGEUS Yes. By the fate of some power we have no children.
MEDEA   Have you a wife, or is there none to share your bed?
AEGEUS There is. Yes, I am joined to my wife in marriage.
MEDEA   And what did Phoebus say to you about children?
AEGEUS Words too wise for a mere man to guess their meaning.
MEDEA   Is it proper for me to be told the god's reply?
AEGEUS It is. For sure what is needed is cleverness.
MEDEA   Then what was his message? Tell me, if I may hear.
AEGEUS I am not to loosen the hanging foot of the wine-skin . . .
MEDEA   Until you have done something, or reached some country?
AEGEUS Until I return again to my hearth and house.
MEDEA   And for what purpose have you journeyed to this land?
AEGEUS There is a man called Pittheus, king of Troezen.
MEDEA   A son of Pelops, they say, a most righteous man.
AEGEUS With him I wish to discuss the reply of the god.
MEDEA   Yes. He is wise and experienced in such matters.
AEGEUS And to me also the dearest of all my spear-friends.
MEDEA   Well, I hope you have good luck, and achieve your will.
AEGEUS But why this downcast eye of yours, and this pale cheek?
MEDEA   O Aegeus, my husband has been the worst of all to me.
AEGEUS What do you mean? Say clearly what has caused this grief.
MEDEA   Jason wrongs me, though I have never injured him.
AEGEUS What has he done? Tell me about it in clearer words.

MEDEA   He has taken a wife to his house, supplanting me.

AEGEUS Surely he would not dare to do a thing like that.

MEDEA   Be sure he has. Once dear, I now am slighted by him.

AEGEUS Did he fall in love? Or is he tired of your love?

MEDEA   He was greatly in love, this traitor to his friends.

AEGEUS Then let him go, if, as you say, he is so bad.

MEDEA   A passionate love—for an alliance with the king.

AEGEUS And who gave him his wife? Tell me the rest of it.

MEDEA   It was Creon, he who rules this land of Corinth.

AEGEUS Indeed, Medea, your grief was understandable.

MEDEA   I am ruined. And there is more to come: I am banished.

AEGEUS Banished? By whom? Here you tell me of a new wrong.

MEDEA   Creon drives me an exile from the land of Corinth.

AEGEUS Does Jason consent? I cannot approve of this.

MEDEA   He pretends not to, but he will put up with it.
        Ah, Aegeus, I beg and beseech you, by your beard
        And by your knees I am making myself your suppliant,
        Have pity on me, have pity on your poor friend,
        And do not let me go into exile desolate,
        But receive me in your land and at your very hearth.
        So may your love, with God's help, lead to the bearing
        Of children, and so may you yourself die happy.
        You do not know what a chance you have come on here.
        I will end your childlessness, and I will make you able
        To beget children. The drugs I know can do this.

AEGEUS For many reasons, woman, I am anxious to do
        This favor for you. First, for the sake of the gods,
        And then for the birth of children which you promise,

For in that respect I am entirely at my wits' end.
But this is my position: if you reach my land,
I, being in my rights, will try to befriend you.
But this much I must warn you of beforehand:
I shall not agree to take you out of this country;
But if you by yourself can reach my house, then you
Shall stay there safely. To none will I give you up
But from this land you must make your escape yourself,
For I do not wish to incur blame from my friends.

MEDEA   It shall be so. But, if I might have a pledge from you
For this, then I would have from you all I desire.

AEGEUS Do you not trust me? What is it rankles with you?

MEDEA   I trust you, yes. But the house of Pelias hates me,
And so does Creon. If you are bound by this oath,
When they try to drag me from your land, you will not
Abandon me; but if our pact is only words,
With no oath to the gods, you will be lightly armed,
Unable to resist their summons. I am weak,
While they have wealth to help them and a royal house.

AEGEUS You show much foresight for such negotiations.
Well, if you will have it so, I will not refuse.
For, both on my side this will be the safest way
To have some excuse to put forward to your enemies,
And for you it is more certain. You may name the gods.

MEDEA   Swear by the plain of Earth, and Helius, father
Of my father, and name together all the gods . . .

AEGEUS That I will act or not act in what way? Speak.

MEDEA   That you yourself will never cast me from your land,
Nor, if any of my enemies should demand me,
Will you, in your life, willingly hand me over.

AEGEUS I swear by the Earth, by the holy light of Helius,
By all the gods, I will abide by this you say.

MEDEA   Enough. And, if you fail, what shall happen to you?

AEGEUS What comes to those who have no regard for heaven.

MEDEA   Go on your way. Farewell. For I am satisfied.
        And I will reach your city as soon as I can,
        Having done the deed I have to do and gained my end.

                                            (*Aegeus goes out.*)

CHORUS May Hermes, god of travelers,
        Escort you, Aegeus, to your home!
        And may you have the things you wish
        So eagerly; for you
        Appear to me to be a generous man.

MEDEA   God, and God's daughter, justice, and light of Helius!
        Now, friends, has come the time of my triumph over
        My enemies, and now my foot is on the road.
        Now I am confident they will pay the penalty.
        For this man, Aegeus, has been like a harbor to me
        In all my plans just where I was most distressed.
        To him I can fasten the cable of my safety
        When I have reached the town and fortress of Pallas.*
        And now I shall tell to you the whole of my plan.
        Listen to these words that are not spoken idly.
        I shall send one of my servants to find Jason
        And request him to come once more into my sight.
        And when he comes, the words I'll say will be soft ones.
        I'll say that I agree with him, that I approve
        The royal wedding he has made, betraying me.
        I'll say it was profitable, an excellent idea.
        But I shall beg that my children may remain here:
        Not that I would leave in a country that hates me
        Children of mine to feel their enemies' insults,
        But that by a trick I may kill the king's daughter.

---

* Athens, the town of Athena.

>   For I will send the children with gifts in their hands
>   To carry to the bride, so as not to be banished—
>   A finely woven dress and a golden diadem.
>   And if she takes them and wears them upon her skin
>   She and all who touch the girl will die in agony;
>   Such poison will I lay upon the gifts I send.
>   But there, however, I must leave that account paid.
>   I weep to think of what a deed I have to do
>   Next after that; for I shall kill my own children.
>   My children, there is none who can give them safety.
>   And when I have ruined the whole of Jason's house,
>   I shall leave the land and flee from the murder of my
>   Dear children, and I shall have done a dreadful deed.
>   For it is not bearable to be mocked by enemies.
>   So it must happen. What profit have I in life?
>   I have no land, no home, no refuge from my pain.
>   My mistake was made the time I left behind me
>   My father's house, and trusted the words of a Greek,
>   Who, with heaven's help, will pay me the price for that.
>   For those children he had from me he will never
>   See alive again, nor will he on his new bride
>   Beget another child, for she is to be forced
>   To die a most terrible death by these my poisons.
>   Let no one think me a weak one, feeble-spirited,
>   A stay-at-home, but rather just the opposite,
>   One who can hurt my enemies and help my friends;
>   For the lives of such persons are most remembered.

CHORUS   Since you have shared the knowledge of your plan with us,
         I both wish to help you and support the normal
         Ways of mankind, and tell you not to do this thing.

MEDEA   I can do no other thing. It is understandable
         For you to speak thus. You have not suffered as I have.

CHORUS   But can you have the heart to kill your flesh and blood?

MEDEA   Yes, for this is the best way to wound my husband.

CHORUS   And you, too. Of women you will be most unhappy.

MEDEA   So it must be. No compromise is possible.

(She turns to the Nurse.)

> Go, you, at once, and tell Jason to come to me.
> You I employ on all affairs of greatest trust.
> Say nothing of these decisions which I have made,
> If you love your mistress, if you were born a woman.

CHORUS   From of old the children of Erechtheus* are
> Splendid, the sons of blessed gods. They dwell
> In Athens' holy and unconquered land,
> Where famous Wisdom feeds them and they pass gaily
> Always through that most brilliant air where once, they say,
> That golden Harmony gave birth to the nine
> Pure Muses of Pieria.

> And beside the sweet flow of Cephisus' stream,**
> Where Cypris sailed, they say, to draw the water,
> And mild soft breezes breathed along her path,
> And on her hair were flung the sweet-smelling garlands
> Of flowers of roses by the Lovers, the companions
> Of Wisdom, her escort, the helpers of men
> In every kind of excellence.

> How then can these holy rivers
> Or this holy land love you,
> Or the city find you a home,
> You, who will kill your children,
> You, not pure with the rest?
> O think of the blow at your children
> And think of the blood that you shed.
> O, over and over I beg you,
> By your knees I beg you do not
> Be the murderess of your babes!

* The Athenians.
** At Athens.

O where will you find the courage
Or the skill of hand and heart,
When you set yourself to attempt
A deed so dreadful to do?
How, when you look upon them,
Can you tearlessly hold the decision
For murder? You will not be able,
When your children fall down and implore you,
You will not be able to dip
Steadfast your hand in their blood.

(Enter Jason with attendants.)

JASON I have come at your request. Indeed, although you are
Bitter against me, this you shall have: I will listen
To what new thing you want, woman, to get from me.

MEDEA Jason, I beg you to be forgiving toward me
For what I said. It is natural for you to bear with
My temper, since we have had much love together.
I have talked with myself about this and I have
Reproached myself. "Fool," I said, "why am I so mad?
Why am I set against those who have planned wisely?
Why make myself an enemy of the authorities
And of my husband, who does the best thing for me
By marrying royalty and having children who
Will be as brothers to my own? What is wrong with me?
Let me give up anger, for the gods are kind to me.
Have I not children, and do I not know that we
In exile from our country must be short of friends?"
When I considered this I saw that I had shown
Great lack of sense, and that my anger was foolish.
Now I agree with you. I think that you are wise
In having this other wife as well as me, and I
Was mad. I should have helped you in these plans of yours,
Have joined in the wedding, stood by the marriage bed,
Have taken pleasure in attendance on your bride.

But we women are what we are—perhaps a little
Worthless; and you men must not be like us in this,
Nor be foolish in return when we are foolish.
Now, I give in, and admit that then I was wrong.
I have come to a better understanding now.

(She turns toward the house.)

Children, come here, my children, come outdoors to us!
Welcome your father with me, and say goodbye to him,
And with your mother, who just now was his enemy,
Join again in making friends with him who loves us.

(Enter the children, attended by the Tutor.)

We have made peace, and all our anger is over.
Take hold of his right hand—O God, I am thinking
Of something which may happen in the secret future.
O children, will you just so, after a long life,
Hold out your loving arms at the grave? O children,
How ready to cry I am, how full of foreboding!
I am ending at last this quarrel with your father,
And look, my soft eyes have suddenly filled with tears.

CHORUS   And the pale tears have started also in my eyes.
O may the trouble not grow worse than now it is!

JASON   I approve of what you say. And I cannot blame you
Even for what you said before. It is natural
For a woman to be wild with her husband when he
Goes in for secret love. But now your mind has turned
To better reasoning. In the end you have come to
The right decision, like the clever woman you are.
And of you, children, your father is taking care.
He has made, with God's help, ample provision for you.
For I think that a time will come when you will be
The leading people in Corinth with your brothers.
You must grow up. As to the future, your father
And those of the gods who love him will deal with that.
I want to see you, when you have become young men,

Healthy and strong, better men than my enemies.
Medea, why are your eyes all wet with pale tears?
Why is your cheek so white and turned away from me?
Are not these words of mine pleasing for you to hear?

MEDEA   It is nothing. I was thinking about these children.

JASON   You must be cheerful. I shall look after them well.

MEDEA   I will be. It is not that I distrust your words,
But a woman is a frail thing, prone to crying.

JASON   But why then should you grieve so much for these children?

MEDEA   I am their mother. When you prayed that they might live
I felt unhappy to think that these things will be.
But come, I have said something of the things I meant
To say to you, and now I will tell you the rest.
Since it is the king's will to banish me from here—
And for me, too, I know that this is the best thing,
Not to be in your way by living here or in
The king's way, since they think me ill-disposed to them—
I then am going into exile from this land;
But do you, so that you may have the care of them,
Beg Creon that the children may not be banished.

JASON   I doubt if I'll succeed, but still I'll attempt it.

MEDEA   Then you must tell your wife to beg from her father
That the children may be reprieved from banishment.

JASON   I will, and with her I shall certainly succeed.

MEDEA   If she is like the rest of us women, you will.
And I, too, will take a hand with you in this business,
For I will send her some gifts which are far fairer,
I am sure of it, than those which now are in fashion,
A finely woven dress and a golden diadem,
And the children shall present them. Quick, let one of you
Servants bring here to me that beautiful dress.

(One of her attendants goes into the house.)

She will be happy not in one way, but in a hundred,
Having so fine a man as you to share her bed,
And with this beautiful dress which Helius of old,
My father's father, bestowed on his descendants.

(Enter attendant carrying the poisoned dress and diadem.)

There, children, take these wedding presents in your hands.
Take them to the royal princess, the happy bride,
And give them to her. She will not think little of them.

JASON No, don't be foolish, and empty your hands of these.
Do you think the palace is short of dresses to wear?
Do you think there is no gold there? Keep them, don't give them
Away. If my wife considers me of any value,
She will think more of me than money, I am sure of it.

MEDEA No, let me have my way. They say the gods themselves
Are moved by gifts, and gold does more with men than words.
Hers is the luck, her fortune that which god blesses;
She is young and a princess; but for my children's reprieve
I would give my very life, and not gold only.
Go children, go together to that rich palace,
Be suppliants to the new wife of your father,
My lady, beg her not to let you be banished.
And give her the dress—for this is of great importance,
That she should take the gift into her hand from yours.
Go, quick as you can. And bring your mother good news
By your success of those things which she longs to gain.

(Jason goes out with his attendants, followed by the Tutor and the children carrying the poisoned gifts.)

CHORUS Now there is no hope left for the children's lives.
Now there is none. They are walking already to murder.

The bride, poor bride, will accept the curse of the gold,
Will accept the bright diadem.
Around her yellow hair she will set that dress
Of death with her own hands.

The grace and the perfume and glow of the golden robe
Will charm her to put them upon her and wear the wreath,
And now her wedding will be with the dead below,
Into such a trap she will fall,
Poor thing, into such a fate of death and never
Escape from under that curse.
You, too, O wretched bridegroom, making your match with kings,
You do not see that you bring
Destruction on your children and on her,
Your wife, a fearful death.
Poor soul, what a fall is yours!

In your grief, too, I weep, mother of little children,
You who will murder your own,
In vengeance for the loss of married love
Which Jason has betrayed
As he lives with another wife.

(*Enter the Tutor with the children.*)

TUTOR   Mistress, I tell you that these children are reprieved,
And the royal bride has been pleased to take in her hands
Your gifts. In that quarter the children are secure.
But come,
Why do you stand confused when you are fortunate?
Why have you turned round with your cheek away from me?
Are not these words of mine pleasing for you to hear?

MEDEA   Oh! I am lost!

TUTOR   That word is not in harmony with my tidings.

MEDEA	I am lost, I am lost!
TUTOR	Am I in ignorance telling you Of some disaster, and not the good news I thought?
MEDEA	You have told what you have told. I do not blame you.
TUTOR	Why then this downcast eye, and this weeping of tears?
MEDEA	Oh, I am forced to weep, old man. The gods and I, I in a kind of madness, have contrived all this.
TUTOR	Courage! You, too, will be brought home by your children.
MEDEA	Ah, before that happens I shall bring others home.
TUTOR	Others before you have been parted from their children. Mortals must bear in resignation their ill luck.
MEDEA	That is what I shall do. But go inside the house, And do for the children your usual daily work.

(The Tutor goes into the house. Medea turns to her children.)

O children, O my children, you have a city,
You have a home, and you can leave me behind you,
And without your mother you may live there forever.
But I am going in exile to another land
Before I have seen you happy and taken pleasure in you,
Before I have dressed your brides and made your marriage
    beds
And held up the torch at the ceremony of wedding.
Oh, what a wretch I am in this my self-willed thought!
What was the purpose, children, for which I reared you?
For all my travail and wearing myself away?
They were sterile, those pains I had in the bearing of you.
Oh surely once the hopes in you I had, poor me,
Were high ones: you would look after me in old age,
And when I died would deck me well with your own hands;
A thing which all would have done. Oh but now it is gone,

That lovely thought. For, once I am left without you,
Sad will be the life I'll lead and sorrowful for me.
And you will never see your mother again with
Your dear eyes, gone to another mode of living.
Why, children, do you look upon me with your eyes?
Why do you smile so sweetly that last smile of all?
Oh, Oh, what can I do? My spirit has gone from me,
Friends, when I saw that bright look in the children's eyes.
I cannot bear to do it. I renounce my plans
I had before. I'll take my children away from
This land. Why should I hurt their father with the pain
They feel, and suffer twice as much of pain myself?
No, no, I will not do it. I renounce my plans.
Ah, what is wrong with me? Do I want to let go
My enemies unhurt and be laughed at for it?
I must face this thing. Oh, but what a weak woman
Even to admit to my mind these soft arguments.
Children, go into the house. And he whom law forbids
To stand in attendance at my sacrifices,
Let him see to it. I shall not mar my handiwork.
Oh! Oh!
Do not, O my heart, you must not do these things!
Poor heart, let them go, have pity upon the children.
If they live with you in Athens they will cheer you.
No! By Hell's avenging furies it shall not be—
This shall never be, that I should suffer my children
To be the prey of my enemies' insolence.
Every way is it fixed. The bride will not escape.
No, the diadem is now upon her head, and she,
The royal princess, is dying in the dress, I know it.
But—for it is the most dreadful of roads for me
To tread, and them I shall send on a more dreadful still—
I wish to speak to the children.

(She calls the children to her.)

                    Come, children, give
Me your hands, give your mother your hands to kiss them.
Oh the dear hands, and oh how dear are these lips to me,
And the generous eyes and the bearing of my children!
I wish you happiness, but not here in this world.
What is here your father took. Oh how good to hold you!
How delicate the skin, how sweet the breath of children!
Go, go! I am no longer able, no longer
To look upon you. I am overcome by sorrow.

(The children go into the house.)

I know indeed what evil I intend to do,
But stronger than all my afterthoughts is my fury,
Fury that brings upon mortals the greatest evils.

(She goes out to the right, toward the royal palace.)

CHORUS Often before
I have gone through more subtle reasons,
And have come upon questionings greater
Than a woman should strive to search out.
But we too have a goddess to help us
And accompany us into wisdom.
Not all of us. Still you will find
Among many women a few,
And our sex is not without learning.
This I say, that those who have never
Had children, who know nothing of it,
In happiness have the advantage
Over those who are parents.
The childless, who never discover
Whether children turn out as a good thing
Or as something to cause pain, are spared
Many troubles in lacking this knowledge.
And those who have in their homes
The sweet presence of children, I see that their lives

Are all wasted away by their worries.
First they must think how to bring them up well and
How to leave them something to live on.
And then after this whether all their toil
Is for those who will turn out good or bad,
Is still an unanswered question.
And of one more trouble, the last of all,
That is common to mortals I tell.
For suppose you have found them enough for their living,
Suppose that the children have grown into youth
And have turned out good, still, if God so wills it,
Death will away with your children's bodies,
And carry them off into Hades.
What is our profit, then, that for the sake of
Children the gods should pile upon mortals
After all else
This most terrible grief of all?

(Enter Medea, from the spectators' right.)

MEDEA Friends, I can tell you that for long I have waited
For the event. I stare toward the place from where
The news will come. And now, see one of Jason's servants
Is on his way here, and that labored breath of his
Shows he has tidings for us, and evil tidings.

(Enter, also from the right, the Messenger.)

MESSENGER Medea, you who have done such a dreadful thing,
So outrageous, run for your life, take what you can,
A ship to bear you hence or chariot on land.

MEDEA And what is the reason deserves such flight as this?

MESSENGER She is dead, only just now, the royal princess,
And Creon dead, too, her father, by your poisons.

MEDEA The finest words you have spoken. Now and hereafter
I shall count you among my benefactors and friends.

MESSENGER   What! Are you right in the mind? Are you not mad,
  Woman? The house of the king is outraged by you.
  Do you enjoy it? Not afraid of such doings?

MEDEA   To what you say I on my side have something too
  To say in answer. Do not be in a hurry, friend,
  But speak. How did they die? You will delight me twice
  As much again if you say they died in agony.

MESSENGER   When those two children, born of you, had entered in,
  Their father with them, and passed into the bride's house,
  We were pleased, we slaves who were distressed by your wrongs.
  All through the house we were talking of but one thing,
  How you and your husband had made up your quarrel.
  Some kissed the children's hands and some their yellow hair,
  And I myself was so full of my joy that I
  Followed the children into the women's quarters.
  Our mistress, whom we honor now instead of you,
  Before she noticed that your two children were there,
  Was keeping her eye fixed eagerly on Jason.
  Afterwards, however, she covered up her eyes,
  Her cheek paled, and she turned herself away from him,
  So disgusted was she at the children's coming there.
  But your husband tried to end the girl's bad temper,
  And said, "You must not look unkindly on your friends.
  Cease to be angry. Turn your head to me again.
  Have as your friends the same ones as your husband has.
  And take these gifts, and beg your father to reprieve
  These children from their exile. Do it for my sake."
  She, when she saw the dress, could not restrain herself.
  She agreed with all her husband said, and before
  He and the children had gone far from the palace,
  She took the gorgeous robe and dressed herself in it,
  And put the golden crown around her curly locks,

And arranged the set of the hair in a shining mirror,
And smiled at the lifeless image of herself in it.
Then she rose from her chair and walked about the room,
With her gleaming feet stepping most soft and delicate,
All overjoyed with the present. Often and often
She would stretch her foot out straight and look along it.
But after that it was a fearful thing to see.
The color of her face changed, and she staggered back,
She ran, and her legs trembled, and she only just
Managed to reach a chair without falling flat down.
An aged woman servant who, I take it, thought
This was some seizure of Pan or another god,
Cried out, "God bless us," but that was before she saw
The white foam breaking through her lips and her rolling
The pupils of her eyes and her face all bloodless.
Then she raised a different cry from that "God bless us,"
A huge shriek, and the women ran, one to the king,
One to the newly wedded husband to tell him
What had happened to his bride; and with frequent sound
The whole of the palace rang as they went running.
One walking quickly round the course of a race-track
Would now have turned the bend and be close to the goal,
When she, poor girl, opened her shut and speechless eye,
And with a terrible groan she came to herself.
For a twofold pain was moving up against her.
The wreath of gold that was resting around her head
Let forth a fearful stream of all-devouring fire,
And the finely woven dress your children gave to her,
Was fastening on the unhappy girl's fine flesh.
She leapt up from the chair, and all on fire she ran,
Shaking her hair now this way and now that, trying
To hurl the diadem away; but fixedly
The gold preserved its grip, and, when she shook her hair,
Then more and twice as fiercely the fire blazed out.
Till, beaten by her fate, she fell down to the ground,

Hard to be recognized except by a parent.
Neither the setting of her eyes was plain to see,
Nor the shapeliness of her face. From the top of
Her head there oozed out blood and fire mixed together.
Like the drops on pine-bark, so the flesh from her bones
Dropped away, torn by the hidden fang of the poison.
It was a fearful sight; and terror held us all
From touching the corpse. We had learned from what had
   happened.
But her wretched father, knowing nothing of the event,
Came suddenly to the house, and fell upon the corpse,
And at once cried out and folded his arms about her,
And kissed her and spoke to her, saying, "O my poor child,
What heavenly power has so shamefully destroyed you?
And who has set me here like an ancient sepulcher,
Deprived of you? O let me die with you, my child!"
And when he had made an end of his wailing and crying,
Then the old man wished to raise himself to his feet;
But, as the ivy clings to the twigs of the laurel,
So he stuck to the fine dress, and he struggled fearfully.
For he was trying to lift himself to his knee,
And she was pulling him down, and when he tugged hard
He would be ripping his aged flesh from his bones.
At last his life was quenched, and the unhappy man
Gave up the ghost, no longer could hold up his head.
There they lie close, the daughter and the old father,
Dead bodies, an event he prayed for in his tears.
As for your interests, I will say nothing of them,
For you will find your own escape from punishment.
Our human life I think and have thought a shadow,
And I do not fear to say that those who are held
Wise among men and who search the reasons of things
Are those who bring the most sorrow on themselves.
For of mortals there is no one who is happy.
If wealth flows in upon one, one may be perhaps

Luckier than one's neighbor, but still not happy.

(Exit.)

CHORUS   Heaven, it seems, on this day has fastened many
Evils on Jason, and Jason has deserved them.
Poor girl, the daughter of Creon, how I pity you
And your misfortunes, you who have gone quite away
To the house of Hades because of marrying Jason.

MEDEA   Women, my task is fixed: as quickly as I may
To kill my children, and start away from this land,
And not, by wasting time, to suffer my children
To be slain by another hand less kindly to them.
Force every way will have it they must die, and since
This must be so, then I, their mother, shall kill them.
Oh, arm yourself in steel, my heart! Do not hang back
From doing this fearful and necessary wrong.
Oh, come, my hand, poor wretched hand, and take the sword,
Take it, step forward to this bitter starting point,
And do not be a coward, do not think of them,
How sweet they are, and how you are their mother. Just for
This one short day be forgetful of your children,
Afterward weep; for even though you will kill them,
They were very dear—Oh, I am an unhappy woman!

(With a cry she rushes into the house.)

CHORUS   O Earth, and the far shining
Ray of the Sun, look down, look down upon
This poor lost woman, look, before she raises
The hand of murder against her flesh and blood.
Yours was the golden birth from which
She sprang, and now I fear divine
Blood may be shed by men.
O heavenly light, hold back her hand,

Check her, and drive from out the house
The bloody Fury raised by fiends of Hell.

Vain waste, your care of children;
Was it in vain you bore the babes you loved,
After you passed the inhospitable strait
Between the dark blue rocks, Symplegades?
O wretched one, how has it come,
This heavy anger on your heart,
This cruel bloody mind?
For God from mortals asks a stern
Price for the stain of kindred blood
In like disaster falling on their homes.

(A cry from one of the children is heard.)

CHORUS   Do you hear the cry, do you hear the children's cry?
O you hard heart, O woman fated for evil!

ONE OF THE CHILDREN   *(from within)* What can I do and how escape my mother's hands?

ANOTHER CHILD   *(from within)* O my dear brother, I cannot tell. We are lost.

CHORUS   Shall I enter the house? Oh, surely I should
Defend the children from murder.

A CHILD   *(from within)* O help us, in God's name, for now we need your help.
Now, now we are close to it. We are trapped by the sword.

CHORUS   O your heart must have been made of rock or steel,
You who can kill
With your own hand the fruit of your own womb.
Of one alone I have heard, one woman alone
Of those of old who laid her hands on her children,
Ino, sent mad by heaven when the wife of Zeus
Drove her out from her home and made her wander;

And because of the wicked shedding of blood
Of her own children she threw
Herself, poor wretch, into the sea and stepped away
Over the sea-cliff to die with her two children.
What horror more can be? O women's love,
So full of trouble,
How many evils have you caused already!

(Enter Jason, with attendants.)

JASON   You women, standing close in front of this dwelling,
Is she, Medea, she who did this dreadful deed,
Still in the house, or has she run away in flight?
For she will have to hide herself beneath the earth,
Or raise herself on wings into the height of air,
If she wishes to escape the royal vengeance.
Does she imagine that, having killed our rulers,
She will herself escape uninjured from this house?
But I am thinking not so much of her as for
The children—her the king's friends will make to suffer
For what she did. So I have come to save the lives
Of my boys, in case the royal house should harm them
While taking vengeance for their mother's wicked deed.

CHORUS   O Jason, if you but knew how deeply you are
Involved in sorrow, you would not have spoken so.

JASON   What is it? That she is planning to kill me also?

CHORUS   Your children are dead, and by their own mother's hand.

JASON   What! That is it? O woman, you have destroyed me!

CHORUS   You must make up your mind your children are no more.

JASON   Where did she kill them? Was it here or in the house?

CHORUS   Open the gates and there you will see them murdered.

JASON   Quick as you can unlock the doors, men, and undo
         The fastenings and let me see this double evil,
         My children dead and her—Oh her I will repay.

> (*His attendants rush to the door. Medea appears above the house in a chariot drawn by dragons. She has the dead bodies of the children with her.*)

MEDEA   Why do you batter these gates and try to unbar them,
         Seeking the corpses and for me who did the deed?
         You may cease your trouble, and, if you have need of me,
         Speak, if you wish. You will never touch me with your hand,
         Such a chariot has Helius, my father's father,
         Given me to defend me from my enemies.

JASON   You hateful thing, you woman most utterly loathed
         By the gods and me and by all the race of mankind,
         You who have had the heart to raise a sword against
         Your children, you, their mother, and left me childless—
         You have done this, and do you still look at the sun
         And at the earth, after these most fearful doings?
         I wish you dead. Now I see it plain, though at that time
         I did not, when I took you from your foreign home
         And brought you to a Greek house, you, an evil thing,
         A traitress to your father and your native land.
         The gods hurled the avenging curse of yours on me.
         For your own brother you slew at your own hearthside,
         And then came aboard that beautiful ship, the Argo.
         And that was your beginning. When you were married
         To me, your husband, and had borne children to me,
         For the sake of pleasure in the bed you killed them.
         There is no Greek woman who would have dared such deeds,
         Out of all those whom I passed over and chose you
         To marry instead, a bitter destructive match,

A monster, not a woman, having a nature
Wilder than that of Scylla in the Tuscan sea.*
Ah! no, not if I had ten thousand words of shame
Could I sting you. You are naturally so brazen.
Go, worker in evil, stained with your children's blood.
For me remains to cry aloud upon my fate,
Who will get no pleasure from my newly wedded love,
And the boys whom I begot and brought up, never
Shall I speak to them alive. Oh, my life is over!

MEDEA   Long would be the answer which I might have made to
These words of yours, if Zeus the father did not know
How I have treated you and what you did to me.
No, it was not to be that you should scorn my love,
And pleasantly live your life through, laughing at me;
Nor would the princess, nor he who offered the match,
Creon, drive me away without paying for it.
So now you may call me a monster, if you wish,
A Scylla housed in the caves of the Tuscan sea.
I too, as I had to, have taken hold of your heart.

JASON   You feel the pain yourself. You share in my sorrow.

MEDEA   Yes, and my grief is gain when you cannot mock it.

JASON   O children, what a wicked mother she was to you!

MEDEA   They died from a disease they caught from their father.

JASON   I tell you it was not my hand that destroyed them.

MEDEA   But it was your insolence, and your virgin wedding.

JASON   And just for the sake of that you chose to kill them.

MEDEA   Is love so small a pain, do you think, for a woman?

JASON   For a wise one, certainly. But you are wholly evil.

---

* A monster in the *Odyssey*.

MEDEA   The children are dead. I say this to make you suffer.

JASON   The children, I think, will bring down curses on you.

MEDEA   The gods know who was the author of this sorrow.

JASON   Yes, the gods know indeed, they know your loathsome heart.

MEDEA   Hate me. But I tire of your barking bitterness.

JASON   And I of yours. It is easier to leave you.

MEDEA   How then? What shall I do? I long to leave you too.

JASON   Give me the bodies to bury and to mourn them.

MEDEA   No, that I will not. I will bury them myself,
Bearing them to Hera's temple on the promontory;
So that no enemy may evilly treat them
By tearing up their grave. In this land of Corinth
I shall establish a holy feast and sacrifice
Each year for ever to atone for the blood guilt.
And I myself go to the land of Erechtheus
To dwell in Aegeus' house, the son of Pandion.
While you, as is right, will die without distinction,
Struck on the head by a piece of the Argo's timber,
And you will have seen the bitter end of my love.

JASON   May a Fury for the children's sake destroy you,
And justice, Requitor of blood.

MEDEA   What heavenly power lends an ear
To a breaker of oaths, a deceiver?

JASON   Oh, I hate you, murderess of children.

MEDEA   Go to your palace. Bury your bride.

JASON   I go, with two children to mourn for.

MEDEA   Not yet do you feel it. Wait for the future.

JASON   Oh, children I loved!

MEDEA   I loved them, you did not.

JASON   You loved them, and killed them.

MEDEA   To make you feel pain.

JASON   Oh, wretch that I am, how I long
        To kiss the dear lips of my children!

MEDEA   Now you would speak to them, now you would kiss them.
        Then you rejected them.

JASON   Let me, I beg you,
        Touch my boys' delicate flesh.

MEDEA   I will not. Your words are all wasted.

JASON   O God, do you hear it, this persecution,
        These my sufferings from this hateful
        Woman, this monster, murderess of children?
        Still what I can do that I will do:
        I will lament and cry upon heaven,
        Calling the gods to bear me witness
        How you have killed my boys and prevent me from
        Touching their bodies or giving them burial.
        I wish I had never begot them to see them
        Afterward slaughtered by you.

CHORUS   Zeus in Olympus is the overseer
           Of many doings. Many things the gods
           Achieve beyond our judgment. What we thought
           Is not confirmed and what we thought not god
           Contrives. And so it happens in this story.

(Curtain.)

DOVER · THRIFT · EDITIONS

NONFICTION

NARRATIVE OF THE LIFE OF FREDERICK DOUGLASS, Frederick Douglass. 96pp. 28499-9
SELF-RELIANCE AND OTHER ESSAYS, Ralph Waldo Emerson. 128pp. 27790-9
THE LIFE OF OLAUDAH EQUIANO, OR GUSTAVUS VASSA, THE AFRICAN, Olaudah Equiano. 192pp. 40661-X
THE AUTOBIOGRAPHY OF BENJAMIN FRANKLIN, Benjamin Franklin. 144pp. 29073-5
TOTEM AND TABOO, Sigmund Freud. 176pp. (Not available in Europe or United Kingdom.) 40434-X
LOVE: A Book of Quotations, Herb Galewitz (ed.). 64pp. 40004-2
PRAGMATISM, William James. 128pp. 28270-8
THE STORY OF MY LIFE, Helen Keller. 80pp. 29249-5
TAO TE CHING, Lao Tze. 112pp. 29792-6
GREAT SPEECHES, Abraham Lincoln. 112pp. 26872-1
THE PRINCE, Niccolò Machiavelli. 80pp. 27274-5
THE SUBJECTION OF WOMEN, John Stuart Mill. 112pp. 29601-6
SELECTED ESSAYS, Michel de Montaigne. 96pp. 29109-X
UTOPIA, Sir Thomas More. 96pp. 29583-4
BEYOND GOOD AND EVIL: Prelude to a Philosophy of the Future, Friedrich Nietzsche. 176pp. 29868-X
THE BIRTH OF TRAGEDY, Friedrich Nietzsche. 96pp. 28515-4
COMMON SENSE, Thomas Paine. 64pp. 29602-4
SYMPOSIUM AND PHAEDRUS, Plato. 96pp. 27798-4
THE TRIAL AND DEATH OF SOCRATES: Four Dialogues, Plato. 128pp. 27066-1
A MODEST PROPOSAL AND OTHER SATIRICAL WORKS, Jonathan Swift. 64pp. 28759-9
CIVIL DISOBEDIENCE AND OTHER ESSAYS, Henry David Thoreau. 96pp. 27563-9
SELECTIONS FROM THE JOURNALS (Edited by Walter Harding), Henry David Thoreau. 96pp. 28760-2
WALDEN; OR, LIFE IN THE WOODS, Henry David Thoreau. 224pp. 28495-6
NARRATIVE OF SOJOURNER TRUTH, Sojourner Truth. 80pp. 29899-X
THE THEORY OF THE LEISURE CLASS, Thorstein Veblen. 256pp. 28062-4
DE PROFUNDIS, Oscar Wilde. 64pp. 29308-4
OSCAR WILDE'S WIT AND WISDOM: A Book of Quotations, Oscar Wilde. 64pp. 40146-4
UP FROM SLAVERY, Booker T. Washington. 160pp. 28738-6
A VINDICATION OF THE RIGHTS OF WOMAN, Mary Wollstonecraft. 224pp. 29036-0

PLAYS

PROMETHEUS BOUND, Aeschylus. 64pp. 28762-9
THE ORESTEIA TRILOGY: Agamemnon, The Libation-Bearers and The Furies, Aeschylus. 160pp. 29242-8
LYSISTRATA, Aristophanes. 64pp. 28225-2
WHAT EVERY WOMAN KNOWS, James Barrie. 80pp. (Not available in Europe or United Kingdom.) 29578-8
THE CHERRY ORCHARD, Anton Chekhov. 64pp. 26682-6
THE SEA GULL, Anton Chekhov. 64pp. 40656-3
THE THREE SISTERS, Anton Chekhov. 64pp. 27544-2
UNCLE VANYA, Anton Chekhov. 64pp. 40159-6
THE WAY OF THE WORLD, William Congreve. 80pp. 27787-9
BACCHAE, Euripides. 64pp. 29580-X
MEDEA, Euripides. 64pp. 27548-5

DOVER·THRIFT·EDITIONS

PLAYS

The Mikado, William Schwenck Gilbert. 64pp. 27268-0
Faust, Part One, Johann Wolfgang von Goethe. 192pp. 28046-2
The Inspector General, Nikolai Gogol. 80pp. 28500-6
She Stoops to Conquer, Oliver Goldsmith. 80pp. 26867-5
A Doll's House, Henrik Ibsen. 80pp. 27062-9
Ghosts, Henrik Ibsen. 64pp. 29852-3
Hedda Gabler, Henrik Ibsen. 80pp. 26469-6
The Wild Duck, Henrik Ibsen. 96pp. 41116-8
Volpone, Ben Jonson. 112pp. 28049-7
Dr. Faustus, Christopher Marlowe. 64pp. 28208-2
The Misanthrope, Molière. 64pp. 27065-3
Anna Christie, Eugene O'Neill. 80pp. 29985-6
Beyond the Horizon, Eugene O'Neill. 96pp. 29085-9
The Emperor Jones, Eugene O'Neill. 64pp. 29268-1
The Long Voyage Home and Other Plays, Eugene O'Neill. 80pp. 28755-6
Right You Are, If You Think You Are, Luigi Pirandello. 64pp. (Not available in Europe or United Kingdom.) 29576-1
Six Characters in Search of an Author, Luigi Pirandello. 64pp. (Not available in Europe or United Kingdom.) 29992-9
Phèdre, Jean Racine. 64pp. 41927-4
Hands Around, Arthur Schnitzler. 64pp. 28724-6
Antony and Cleopatra, William Shakespeare. 128pp. 40062-X
As You Like It, William Shakespeare. 80pp. 40432-3
Hamlet, William Shakespeare. 128pp. 27278-8
Henry IV, William Shakespeare. 96pp. 29584-2
Julius Caesar, William Shakespeare. 80pp. 26876-4
King Lear, William Shakespeare. 112pp. 28058-6
Love's Labour's Lost, William Shakespeare. 64pp. 41929-0
Macbeth, William Shakespeare. 96pp. 27802-6
Measure for Measure, William Shakespeare. 96pp. 40889-2
The Merchant of Venice, William Shakespeare. 96pp. 28492-1
A Midsummer Night's Dream, William Shakespeare. 80pp. 27067-X
Much Ado About Nothing, William Shakespeare. 80pp. 28272-4
Othello, William Shakespeare. 112pp. 29097-2
Richard III, William Shakespeare. 112pp. 28747-5
Romeo and Juliet, William Shakespeare. 96pp. 27557-4
The Taming of the Shrew, William Shakespeare. 96pp. 29765-9
The Tempest, William Shakespeare. 96pp. 40658-X
Twelfth Night; or, What You Will, William Shakespeare. 80pp. 29290-8
Arms and the Man, George Bernard Shaw. 80pp. (Not available in Europe or United Kingdom.) 26476-9
Heartbreak House, George Bernard Shaw. 128pp. (Not available in Europe or United Kingdom.) 29291-6
Pygmalion, George Bernard Shaw. 96pp. (Available in U.S. only.) 28222-8
The Rivals, Richard Brinsley Sheridan. 96pp. 40433-1
The School for Scandal, Richard Brinsley Sheridan. 96pp. 26687-7
Antigone, Sophocles. 64pp. 27804-2
Oedipus at Colonus, Sophocles. 64pp. 40659-8
Oedipus Rex, Sophocles. 64pp. 26877-2

DOVER·THRIFT·EDITIONS

PLAYS

ELECTRA, Sophocles. 64pp. 28482-4
MISS JULIE, August Strindberg. 64pp. 27281-8
THE PLAYBOY OF THE WESTERN WORLD AND RIDERS TO THE SEA, J. M. Synge. 80pp. 27562-0
THE DUCHESS OF MALFI, John Webster. 96pp. 40660-1
THE IMPORTANCE OF BEING EARNEST, Oscar Wilde. 64pp. 26478-5
LADY WINDERMERE'S FAN, Oscar Wilde. 64pp. 40078-6

BOXED SETS

FAVORITE JANE AUSTEN NOVELS: *Pride and Prejudice, Sense and Sensibility* and *Persuasion* (Complete and Unabridged), Jane Austen. 800pp. 29748-9
BEST WORKS OF MARK TWAIN: Four Books, Dover. 624pp. 40226-6
EIGHT GREAT GREEK TRAGEDIES: Six Books, Dover. 480pp. 40203-7
FIVE GREAT ENGLISH ROMANTIC POETS, Dover. 496pp. 27893-X
FIVE GREAT PLAYS, Dover. 368pp. 27179-X
47 GREAT SHORT STORIES: Stories by Poe, Chekhov, Maupassant, Gogol, O. Henry, and Twain, Dover. 688pp. 27178-1
GREAT AFRICAN-AMERICAN WRITERS: Seven Books, Dover. 704pp. 29995-3
GREAT AMERICAN NOVELS, Dover. 720pp. 28665-7
GREAT ENGLISH NOVELS, Dover. 704pp. 28666-5
GREAT IRISH WRITERS: Five Books, Dover. 672pp. 29996-1
GREAT MODERN WRITERS: Five Books, Dover. 720pp. (Available in U.S. only.) 29458-7
GREAT WOMEN POETS: 4 Complete Books, Dover. 256pp. (Available in U.S. only.) 28388-7
MASTERPIECES OF RUSSIAN LITERATURE: Seven Books, Dover. 880pp. 40665-2
SEVEN GREAT ENGLISH VICTORIAN POETS: Seven Volumes, Dover. 592pp. 40204-5
SIX GREAT AMERICAN POETS: Poems by Poe, Dickinson, Whitman, Longfellow, Frost, and Millay, Dover. 512pp. (Available in U.S. only.) 27425-X
38 SHORT STORIES BY AMERICAN WOMEN WRITERS: Five Books, Dover. 512pp. 29459-5
26 GREAT TALES OF TERROR AND THE SUPERNATURAL, Dover. 608pp. (Available in U.S. only.) 27891-3

All books complete and unabridged. All 5³⁄₁₆" x 8¼," paperbound. Available at your book dealer, online at **www.doverpublications.com**, or by writing to Dept. GI, Dover Publications, Inc., 31 East 2nd Street, Mineola, NY 11501. For current price information or for free catalogs (please indicate field of interest), write to Dover Publications or log on to **www.doverpublications.com** and see every Dover book in print. Dover publishes more than 500 books each year on science, elementary and advanced mathematics, biology, music, art, literary history, social sciences, and other areas.